WOODLAND
SCENE

Book 1: The Badgers and Brock Manor

M.D.COCKETT

AuthorHouse™ UK
1663 Liberty Drive
Bloomington, IN 47403 USA
www.authorhouse.co.uk
UK TFN: 0800 0148641 (Toll Free inside the UK)
UK Local: 02036 956322 (+44 20 3695 6322 from outside the UK)

Because of the dynamic nature of the Internet, any web addresses or links contained in this book may have changed
since publication and may no longer be valid. The views expressed in this work are solely those of the author and do
not necessarily reflect the views of the publisher, and the publisher hereby disclaims any responsibility for them.

Any people depicted in stock imagery provided by Getty Images are models,
and such images are being used for illustrative purposes only.
Certain stock imagery © Getty Images.

This book is printed on acid-free paper.

ISBN: 978-1-6655-9767-8 (sc)
ISBN: 978-1-6655-9766-1 (e)

Print information available on the last page.

Published by AuthorHouse 03/21/2022

The stories in this book are based on the "Woodland Scene" range of soft-toys designed by
Lin Cockett c1990. The whole range of 18" tall soft-toys patterns can be purchased as "Tip-
Top" Toy Patterns from Cockett Crafts which include detailed making instructions.

Other books containing short stories of each of the other "Woodland Scene" animals are available.

Soft-toy catalogues can be obtained by writing to:-
COCKETT CRAFTS. 1 Ryelands Grove, Leominster.
Herefordshire HR6 8QA
Tel: (01568)-613697

authorHOUSE®

ACKNOWLEDGEMENTS

With thanks to my late wife, Linda (Lin) who designed the wonderful range of collectable soft-toys from which my inspiration was generated to write these stories, and who drew some of the illustrations.

ILLUSTRATIONS

WOODLAND SCENE

Book 1: The Badgers and Brock Manor

by

M.D. COCKETT

CONTENTS

Crash! .... The Weasel's paw came through the broken pane.

CHAPTER 1

THE ATTACK

Bessie Beaver hummed nervously to herself as she bustled along the path on her way to work.

Her eyes were continually searching the sides of the path ahead, and occasionally she reassuringly glanced behind her.

She had walked from her home in Riverside Dwellings to work at Brock Manor countless times before, but today something was different. She could sense something, but could not identify it. She was now the housekeeper at the Manor, but, as she recalled the many happy journeys to and from work, she could *not* remember ever feeling the eerie feeling she felt today.

It was mid-springtime and the flowers were already out, catching the early morning sunshine. The primroses and clusters of crocuses had shrugged off winter and the trumpets of the golden daffodils heralded in the dawn of a beautiful day.

Ugh! She shuddered, as she remembered those recent long dark winters' nights, with the paths covered in frost, which had caused her to slip, and fall twice, into the crispy snow, making her all wet and miserable, as well as cold.

She shrugged her shoulders and quickened her step towards the Manor.

The low morning sun was casting a long shadow of herself, which followed just behind her, and no matter how quickly she hurried, she could not get away from it. The thought of it chasing her sent shivers down her back.

"Frightened of my own shadow?" she chuckled nervously to herself. "What a silly old thing I am."

Then she stopped dead in her tracks. A rustling in the undergrowth just to the right in front of her, made her heart pound rapidly in her chest.

Her eager eyes scanned the wayside, and focused on a wrinkled nose which slowly appeared, followed by two piercing eyes.

The face suddenly revealed itself, causing her to start.

"Oh! Hullo, Nattering Jack Toad." she said in a much relieved voice.

"Keep out of sight," was the reply, or was it, "Keep to the right". He did mumble so. It might even have been: "Keen for the fight?" She was in such a state that she was not at all sure what he had said.

She did not want to stop and discuss it with him, as he had already made her late twice that week with his idle nattering.

Composing herself, she hurried on by him, completely forgetting her manners, by not wishing him a good-day, which she always did.

"That's gratitude for you!" muttered Jack, "Oh well, that's the youngsters of today, no time for us old ones. Well at least I tried to warn her."

He looked up after Bessie, but she had already disappeared towards Brock Manor.

When inside the Manor, Bessie slipped off her coat and hat, and was hanging them up, when Perkins the Butler, a wiry old Pine-Marten, wished her politely, "Good-Morning Ma'am. Lovely day. Hope you are well." He said it every morning.

"Yes," she agreed. Well, *he* appeared as though everything was normal, so perhaps it was just herself.

She wished him a good-day, but she still had a very uneasy feeling.

The servants were gathered and she made sure that everyone knew what their jobs were. *They* all seemed to be calm and normal, so she set about her own work.

Spring cleaning had just started. It was the turn of the Library today. Then there was the usual morning shopping, washing and ironing to do, and in between, she had to keep an eye on Sir Regnault, the owner of the Manor.

He was getting old now. In her minds' eye, she recalled his youth, when she was also young, and was saddened to see how such a sprightly young Badger had become old and bed-bound.

Still, he'd had a fine life.

She'd spent a lot of her time recently, nursing the Badger after his fall, while hunting.

Apparently what had happened was, he had tried to hurdle a small hedge, but his horse had slipped in the mud, throwing Sir Regnault into a ditch. The horse then crashed into the snow-covered hedge, dislodging its canopy of snow, which had buried Sir Regnault. By the time he was found, he was cold, thoroughly wet through, and shivering and sneezing, incessantly.

He wasn't going to miss the Hunt Ball that evening though, and would not take any advice about going to bed early, to recover.

Hunt Balls always lasted into the early hours of the next day, and the effect of the soaking from the cold snow, and the late night, soon sapped the Old Badger's energy reserves, and his cold developed into a severe chill. He was ordered to bed, to rest and recover.

That was nearly three months ago, and still there was no sign of any improvement. Bessie had nursed Sir Regnault all that time and had found him to be a very difficult patient.

He would *not* stay in his warm bed, and refused all medical advice, and now he was weak and quite ill. He kept saying, that all he needed, was his Brandy, - for medicinal purposes of course, - but Bessie was quite sure that he was consuming far more than the 'occasional sip'!

Although she searched everywhere in his room, she could not find out where he kept his supplies. All advice to keep warm and quiet were ignored by the Badger. Sir Regnault was the most stubborn Badger ever!

Bessie had written to his two sons, to tell them of Sir Regnault's illness, but the Badgers were not a close family and, so far, neither had even bothered to reply to her letters or enquire about his health.

Bessie often thought how lucky she was, with her family around her, poor as they were in financial terms, but they were *very* rich in family security, and she had noticed how lonely the old Badger had become.

His wealth had not kept *his* family together! As soon as they were able to, both his sons had left home.

Bastien, the younger son, had left the Manor under strange circumstances which no-one talked about, whilst Basil, the elder son, had made a name for himself in business in the City.

Even Sir Regnault's so called friends were not very interested in his health. He had no *real* friends, they were just acquaintances, who only enjoyed his hospitality, his parties, and his social meetings.

This morning, Bessie felt that she had to keep a rather watchful eye on her master, as he had not looked too well when she had first visited him. It was now 10:45, almost time for their morning break for their 'elevenses'.

The kettle had been filled with water, the cups were ready, with milk, sugar and spoons laid out, waiting for the kettle to boil. She just had time to visit Sir Regnault.

She climbed the stairs, wishing she had a penny for the number of times she had climbed those stairs recently, and was brought back to reality by a series of dull moans and groans coming from Sir Regnault's bedroom.

Bessie tip-toed to the door, knocked lightly, waited a few seconds, then opened the door slowly and peered round the door.

Sir Regnault was not in his bed!

Her eyes searched round the room quickly. She could see nothing, but she could hear a soft moaning noise coming from the other side of the bed.

She found Sir Regnault between the curtains and the window, all doubled up in pain.

"Whatever is the matter?" she asked calmly and quietly, "I think you should really be in bed."

"Never mind that now," gestured the Badger at the window, "Look out there."

"You'll catch your death," she mumbled to him as her eyes followed the direction of his trembling fingers.

Several Weasels were slowly coming across the croquet lawn, some of them were pulling a huge wooden object, which she did not recognize.

As it squeaked and rattled closer to the Manor, some Weasels were shouting. "Pull! Pull! Pull!" and others, "Push! Push! Push!"

Some of the puffing pushers and the panting pullers were muttering. "Why can't they make up their minds what we're supposed to be doing!"

Sir Regnault had obviously heard the commotion as he laid in his bed and had got out to see what the disturbance was.

"What do you make of it Bessie dear?" he enquired in a painful voice.

"Don't you worry yourself about them," said Bessie.

"But what are they doing? Do you recognize any of them?"

Bessie looked again through the window, this time more acutely.

By now the object had cut two wheel tracks across the soft croquet lawn, and it was almost up to the house. She dare not tell Sir Regnault that, for the croquet lawn was his pride and joy. A group of four Weasels were pulling on a rope and another three had opened the top of the huge dustbin-like object that they had all been moving.

Inside the contraption were two more Weasels, and they were extending a ladder, - yes it was definitely a ladder, - and the top of the ladder was moving slowly but surely, towards the very window Bessie was looking out of.

"Have you asked for the gutters to be emptied or the windows to be cleaned?" she asked the old Badger.

"Definitely not!" came the angry reply, "What the devil is going on? Why do you ask?

"Well, there are several Weasels just below your window with a large dustbin and there is a ladder coming up to this window."

She regretted saying that, because it sounded quite ridiculous, and she feared the old Badger might explode with rage.

But he didn't. He just lay on the bed and groaned.

Just at that moment a rattle at the window startled Bessie.

It was the face of a Weasel with wicked little eyes - Ugh! She hated Weasels - and in his mouth was a rusty old sword, the handle of which was tapping the window.

"Ooooopen theeeeees veeeeendow," he demanded, through his clenched teeth.

Bessie shrugged her shoulders, "I can't understand what you're saying," she said.

The Weasel opened his mouth to repeat his order, and the sword fell, clanging and clattering, into the dustbin-like contraption below.

"Be careful!" came a frightened voice from below, "You almost killed me."

The Weasel at the top of the ladder glanced at Bessie, his eyes blaming her for making him drop the sword, then he disappeared as quickly as he had appeared, retrieved the sword, and, with it tucked in his belt this time, climbed up to the window again.

This time Bessie could clearly hear his demand to open the window.

"Certainly not." she said, "Do you have an appointment?"- Her training was immaculate. - "No one enters the manor without an appointment, you know."

Crash! The window pane was shattered, showering glass into the room. The Weasel's paw came through the broken pane, curling round the woodwork to find the catch.

As the Weasel fumbled with the catch, Sir Regnault jumped out of his bed, grabbed the nearest thing to him, which happened to be his shooting stick, and began beating away at the intruding arm.

The shooting stick broke with the force of the blows, and sweet-smelling Brandy spilt all over the window.

With an ear-piercing screech, the Weasel fell backwards onto more Weasels, who were climbing up the ladder. All the Weasels then fell, in a crumpled mass of wriggling, screaming bodies, into the contraption, and around it.

The window was closed and the catch was secured and Sir Regnault, for once in his life, showed some consideration for others and asked Bessie if she was all right.

"I'm O.K." replied Bessie. "It had all happened too quickly for me to think about being frightened. What on earth is going on?"

The old Badger sat back on his bed, let out a sigh of relief and said, "I suppose you had better know the whole story."

"Last week I received a letter from them blessed Weasels. They demanded that I give them some of our property, next to the river, so that they could build more homes. I told them that I would not sell under any circumstances."

"They said they did not want to buy it, and would take it by force if I didn't let them have it."

"Over my dead body," I told them. "Who do they think they are?"

"But they can't do that," said Bessie.

Just at that moment a horrible smell wafted into the bedroom, instantly recognized by Bessie.

"Oh, my goodness!" she cried, "The kettle has boiled dry. The staff will have no tea."

She hurried down the stairs, shouting to Silvia Shrew to take the kettle off the stove, but Silvia didn't answer.

She had joined all the staff outside, seeing what the noise was all about, and they were all staring at the mass of squealing Weasels and the damage to the croquet lawn.

Bobby Bunny, the gardener, had just arrived to join the gathering by the front door, and was carrying his garden fork.

With the Weasels in their state of confusion, Bobby raised his garden fork over his head, and ran towards them shouting, "Charge!"

The dazed Weasels looked up, not quite sure what to do.

When they saw the bounding Bunny coming towards them, with a raised garden folk in his hands, they panicked.

"Retreat!" one of them screamed, and they all rose as one, scrambled to their feet and fled as quickly as their little legs would carry them. They ran off in all directions, gripped by the fear of being caught by Bobby Bunny and his garden fork.

Somehow they all managed to flee down the path and out of the grounds, chased by Bobby brandishing his garden fork.

Bobby Bunny returned, quite out-of-breath, to the Manor, and was helped into the kitchen, but the smell left from the burning kettle was too much, so all the servants were ushered into the Main Hall for their elevenses, even though it was nearly lunch-time by now.

Bobby Bunny removed his dirty shoes as he always did, to keep any mud on his shoes, off the newly cleaned floors.

Bessie, by now, had found another old kettle and was lifting the lid, to fill it with water, when a piece of folded paper fell out, and onto the floor.

She bent down to pick it up, as the kettle was filling. It looked like an old letter. She tucked it into her apron pocket to look at later, for the staff were all waiting for their tea.

Of course, all anyone talked about was the invasion by the Weasels. They all had their own opinions as to why the Weasels should want to attack the Manor, but only Bessie knew the real reason and her immaculate training had taught her not to divulge any information to the staff.

When asked for her opinion, she hesitated, before saying that she really had no idea. The rest of the household guessed that she was hiding something, knowing that Sir Regnault had probably confided in her for she had a way of getting people to tell her their secrets, without them even realizing they had done so.

By now the Cuckoo clock had struck 12 times, indicating lunch time was only an hour away. It made Bessie sit up with a start, as she was thinking about her walk to work that morning.

She gave orders that the rubbish left by the invading Weasels should be cleared by Bobby Bunny, and the mess left in the kitchen by the burning kettle, was to be cleaned up by Silvia Shrew, because she had left the kettle unattended.

A sentry was posted near the gates in case the Weasels decided to try to recover their contraption or mount a fresh attack.

"I don't think that's necessary, even Weasels aren't stupid enough to attack again in broad daylight", stated Bobby Bunny, in his "I stopped the invasion" manner. Nevertheless the sentry *was* posted.

In the afternoon, Bessie took one of the maids shopping with her for company, in case the Weasels decided to attack her.

Bessie said to her companion, "It's a funny thing, but on my way into work this morning, I kept having eerie feelings and thinking something was wrong, and when the Cuckoo clock struck twelve o'clock, I suddenly realized what it was. - There were no birds singing this morning!

The Weasels must have been close to the path she had taken to work that day.

Birds, like Beavers, don't like Weasels.

Perhaps if she had spent a few minutes with Nattering Jack Toad, and queried what he had said, then the invasion might have been avoided, the kettle would not have burned, and she could have gone shopping in the morning, but she would not have discovered where Sir Regnault hid his Brandy, neither would she have found the old letter in the old kettle.

That evening she went home quickly, and still the birds were not singing and she had quite forgotten about the folded letter still tucked in her apron pocket!

Bastien stood there .... quite disheveled and muddy

CHAPTER 2

THE HOMECOMING

A few days after the attack by the Weasels, things were returning to normal, and the birds were singing their choruses in the mornings to accompany Bessie to work.

Sir Regnault was still not his normal self, getting more irritable each day, as he was slow to recover from his chill.

Bessie was now quite used to his moans and groans and the window pane had been repaired thanks to a very patient Ozzie (Odd-job) the Otter.

Every little scrape, to remove the old putty from around the broken pane, the slight draught when the broken pane was finally removed, and the smell of fresh linseed oil in the new putty, had all prompted Sir Regnault to find cause to complain.

But Ozzie had been very patient and completed the work. After all, the longer the job took, the more he got paid!

A letter had at last arrived from Bastien, the younger son of Sir Regnault, which said he would come to visit his father when he could raise enough money for the fare, or find a lift with someone who was travelling in the direction of the Manor.

"It's amazing," said Sir Regnault, "all that allowance money I send him each month, and he can't find the fare to visit his own father! What does he do with it all?"

Bessie was pleased to hear that Bastien might appear any day. She had been with the household when he was small and they were good friends.

She knew what he did with his money. He, like his father, had expensive friends.

She knew all about his big house and parties.

He had spent a lot of money buying his house, and also had earned a lot from deals at the Stock Exchange.

But what he earned, he spent on having a very enjoyable time. He always seemed to survive. He would only contact home if he was desperate for money and always the Old Badger sent him more.

He must have been doing reasonably well recently, as the household had not heard from Bastien for quite some time now.

They had seen his name, associated with others, in the society columns of the national newspapers. The last reported sighting was with a Pop-star, Miss Krissy Katze, of a foreign singing group called the "Katzen Doggz".

The reports all said that Bastien had become the manager of the group. "What did he know about the pop world?" Bessie wondered.

She did not like to interfere with the Badgers' domestic problems, but she regularly sent Bastien letters about the local news, so he was well aware of the attack on the Manor and of his father's poor health.

It was another three weeks before a knock came at the back door of the Manor, and Bastien stood there with no luggage, just the clothes he stood up in, looking quite disheveled and muddy.

He had managed to get a lift most of the way, but had had to walk the last three miles across the fields to the Manor itself.

"You took your time in getting here," was the only greeting he received from his father.

"It was quite difficult getting away from my business duties," said Bastien, through gritted teeth.

Most believed that he was a coward and did not want to see his father ill, nor get involved with the Weasels, so he had waited until things had quietened down, before coming home.

He had never got on well with his father, for they were too much alike. Both liked a free and easy life of fun, with no decisions to make. Go where you will. Do what you like. Who cares anyway?

But his father had always tried to get Bastien involved with the running of the Manor, as, although Bastien was the younger of Sir Regnault's two sons, and would not legally inherit the Manor, Sir Regnault wanted Bastien to have it.

He was always saying to Bastien: "One day all this will be yours and you must know how to run the estate or else it will fall into rack and ruin."

Bastien was not the slightest bit interested. He loved his own free and easy life.

Within a week of Bastien's return, Sir Regnault died. There was much mourning at the Manor and the solicitors read out the Will after a peaceful funeral.

Practically everything had been left to Bastien as Sir Regnault had always said. The lands, property and the title of "Lord of the Manor" were all his.

The eldest son, Basil, had inherited nothing!

Basil was furious. After all, he *was* the eldest son and had naturally expected everything to be left to him when his father died.

Basil was known locally as "Boots". He got that nickname because, as a young Badger, he could always be found walking round the estate in his father's shoes or slippers and even his great big outdoor boots.

Not long after he was able to walk, he had managed to get both his little legs into one boot and made everybody laugh as he kept falling over trying to follow his father.

Soon after the Will had been read out to the family, Basil returned to the big city and his job as an Estate Agent.

He had made a lot of money buying and selling houses. At one time he even tried to sell Brock Manor, his own home, without even telling his father.

Imagine what Sir Regnault must have thought when some animals turned up on his doorstep saying they wanted to buy the Manor and that they'd been sent by Basil!

Sir Regnault hadn't thought much of that at all!

Basil's only ambition in life was to make money, lots of money, and he didn't care how he did it.

He had become so greedy over the possession of money, that he was quite unbearable to live with and *very* bossy, and the household were clearly relieved when he decided to return to the city.

Sir Regnault had an sister, Blanche Badger, who lived near the city and it was her who had encouraged Basil to become an Estate Agent. Basil called on his Aunt and told her of the Will and how Bastien had inherited the Manor and they were both furious.

Blanche had ambitions of living in the Manor herself, and had expected Basil to inherit it, then, as he would be engrossed in his work making money, she could move into the Manor to look after it for him.

"The Manor is yours by right," stated his Aunt Blanche, "as you are the eldest, and I will do my best to get the decision challenged so that it *will* be yours."

They discussed how this was to be achieved for hours until they finally came up with the solution.

It would be no good going to a solicitor, as the Will of Sir Regnault could not be contested, for he had been the local magistrate and made all the local laws himself.

No! They had to think of some underhanded solution, outside of any laws.

The Weasels held the key to the solution.

Both Basil and his Aunt Blanche were aware of the attack by the Weasels and thought it would be the ideal way of getting Bastien out of the manor, if they could find a way of getting the Weasels to attack the Manor again.

They knew Bastien would run at the first sign of trouble, as he was such a coward.

A devilish plan was conceived and Aunt Blanche was soon writing a letter.

The entrance to the secret tunnel was not hard to find.

CHAPTER 3

BASTIEN IMPRESSES

At last, Blanche Badger had received a reply to her letter, from Wilf Weasel. Yes, the Weasels would help her.

As Bastien was now the Lord of the Manor, following the death of his father, Sir Regnault, they felt it would be easier to get the land they wanted for building.

They had tried to attack the Manor before, but had been chased off by Bobby Bunny and his garden fork, and they had been planning another attack for some time now.

Basil (Boots) Badger promised them that he would tell them of a secret way into the Manor which should make their attack successful. The only condition was, that they let him become the Lord of the Manor, which he said was his by right, as he was older than his brother Bastien, who had inherited the manor through Sir Regnault's Will.

The Weasels were not interested in the Manor, only the field next to the river. Little did they realize, that if they owned the Manor, then they would own the field they wanted - and many others as well.

It was agreed that a letter showing the secret entrance should be sent and the date for the attack mutually agreed.

Basil and his Aunt Blanche were pleased with themselves, for they had got the Weasels willing to do their dirty work. The Weasels would attack the Manor, drive Bastien out, and then they could then take possession.

They sent the letter to Wilf Weasel, explaining the plan, enclosing the map showing the position of the secret entrance into the Manor, and suggesting the best time to attack.

Wilf received the letter, but could not read. In fact, the only person in the family that could read, was his daughter, Winnie Weasel, and she was away for the weekend making plans for a holiday in Dun-hopping-by-the-Sea.

When she returned home, later that day, Wilf asked her to read the letter out to him.

The whole family were eagerly gathered round, as they didn't normally receive letters, and now they had had two close together. It was therefore quite an occasion for them.

They looked at the little envelope as it lay on the table. Everyone had to touch it, then someone said they ought to open it.

The envelope was handed with great ceremony to Winnie, who tore open the flap, making everyone gasp with horror. They thought she had torn the letter up!

It read: To Wilfred Weasel.
    Old Fox Holes.
    Nearsum.
    Brocks.

    Dear Mr Weasel,
    Further to our talk about both our problems, we enclose the map of you know what, so that you can get into you know where and get rid of you know who.

    Yours hopefully.

    B. (B). B.   p.s. please find a map enclosed.

Winnie read the letter out loud again. Whatever did it mean?

The other Weasels all looked at the letter. None could read, but they all felt quite important just holding it and looking at the writing.

Willie explained that this was their chance to get the land they wanted to build more urgently needed homes. He referred to the failed attempt to attack the Manor, and told them that there was a secret way into the Manor. The map with the letter showed them where it was.

They reminded *him* of Bobby Bunny and his garden fork. They didn't want to be chased by *him* again.

Wilf explained that, because of the secret entrance shown on the map, they would be able to get into the Manor without even seeing Bobby Bunny, or his fork!

"Now *nobody* is to tell *anybody* outside the family about this letter or map, or of our plans to capture the Manor. Is that clear?" snarled Wilf. "If anybody talks, our surprise attack will no longer be a surprise."

There was a long stony silence and nobody spoke, but they all nodded slowly, and the letter was put behind the clock on the mantlepiece. As the letter was quite a treasure, being only the second one they had ever received, one of the Weasels would, from time to time, remove it from behind the clock, look at it, then put it back, feeling ever so important to have received a letter.

The young Wispy Weasel was so impressed with the letter that he took it out of the envelope and tucked it into his trouser pocket. Then he carefully put the envelope back behind the clock, so nobody would know that the contents were missing.

He went out to play with his friends, and they played head-over-heels and roly-poly down the bank, but the letter fell out of his pocket and was found by Basher Bunny.

Basher liked to pick up things, that others had dropped, as he felt that somebody had to keep the place clean.

That evening at the Warren, Beattie found the letter in Basher's pocket and showed it to her husband, Bobby Bunny. They read through the letter together and thought it was a children's riddle.

They questioned Basher about the letter, where had he found it, and whose it was, but all he said was that he couldn't remember. Beattie knew he *always* played with the Weasels.

Basher had been scolded so many times before, for picking things up off the ground that he wasn't going to tell his parents, as he would only be told off again. He was sent to bed anyway! He decided the best thing to do was to take the letter back to the Weasels, and slip it back into Wispy Weasel's pocket, before he realized that he had lost it.

Bobby Bunny was reading through the local newspaper, the "Woodland Scene", and looking at the advertisements for making garden ponds, when he suddenly jumped out of his chair and said excitedly to Beattie:

"B. (B). B. B. (B). B. - I know who it's from - It's Basil."

"Whatever are you talking about?" said Beattie, quite startled by his outburst and wondering what had happened to make him suddenly speak out. Normally, when he was behind the newspaper, you couldn't get any conversation out of him at all.

"B. (B). B." said Bobby, "In the letter, you know, the one you found in Basher's pocket. I bet the "B. (B). B. is Bastien's brother Basil."

"Why should it be?" asked Beattie.

She received no reply, for Bobby had disappeared without his coat, leaving the door wide open behind him (so she knew he was in a hurry) and she saw him heading towards Brock Manor.

At the Manor, Bobby burst in through the doors, barging past Perkins the Butler, without apologizing and nearly knocking the Pine-Marten over. Then he headed straight for Bastien's study.

He gabbled the story about the letter to Bastien, who calmed him down by saying, "Look here, sit down old chap. Take a big breath and let's go through this slowly, from the top.

Bobby calmed down, then told Bastien about the letter which was found in his son's pocket, what it roughly said and of the signature at the bottom "B. (B). B."

Bastien was no fool. "I think you may be right." he said slowly. "It is likely that the letter came from the Weasels, because they play with your son. It could easily have fallen out of a Weasel's pocket. They attacked us once before and, thanks to you and your garden fork, they failed."

"I also have little doubt that Basil wants me out of the Manor so that he can take over, and I bet Aunt Blanche is behind all this. I have an idea where the secret entrance is, and I suggest we both go and see if there has been any sign of anyone trying to find it.

The entrance to the secret tunnel was not difficult to find. It was close to the garden shed where Bastien had remembered.

Bobby was quite impressed with Bastien's calm reaction to the situation. He certainly was not the coward that everyone had believed him to be. He had been quiet, calm and very collected, and had thought through the problem with great professionalism.

"What we must do," said Bastien, "is to set a trap and catch them in it. Have you any suggestions?"

They discussed some ideas for a sometime and finally came to an agreement.

A huge furry shape suddenly appeared at the entrance ....

CHAPTER 4

THE SECRET ENTRANCE

Two days after the meeting between Bastien Badger and Bobby Bunny, the trap was set.

Bobby was asked not to say anything about their plan to anybody, except an animal who could be thoroughly trusted. Bobby nominated his eldest son, Bertie.

They took turns patrolling near the secret entrance, to see if there was anything unusual happening there. It was easy for Bobby to keep an eye on the area, as he was the Head Gardener and it was his job to walk round the gardens making sure everything was growing to plan anyway.

Bertie was given a job near the secret entrance, tidying up the massive garden, so he could keep watch as well without it being obvious that they were watching the secret entrance.

When work was done and the sun had set, Bastien always went to his new study.

The animals of the household thought it was strange of him to move his study from its normal cozy surrounds, to a little cove next to the kitchen, but they never asked why he had moved there, as Bastien sometimes did unusual things.

Each evening, Bastien could be found with a load of fur-fabric, and an old sewing machine, apparently making soft-toys. The household were curious, and discussed it among themselves, but never mentioned it to him.

A few days passed and everyone was quite used to Bastien's new study and his toy-making and nobody mentioned it any more.

The Weasels had not suspected that the letter from B. (B). B. had been lost, because Basher Bunny had managed to put the letter back into Wispy Weasel's pocket with-out being noticed. Wispy had returned the letter to its envelope the same evening, and no-one knew it had been missing.

The Weasels were now ready. It was two o'clock in the morning and they were armed with their weapons, the map and some torches.

They set off quietly, and soon arrived at the boundary wall of the Manor. It was quite dark because the moon beams could not get through the thick cloudy sky, but there was just enough light for them to recognize where they were. They did not use their torches as someone might see the lights and raise the alarm.

They slid over the boundary wall, crawled towards the secret entrance, and stopped about ten feet from the wall of Brock Manor.

They looked quite frightening, with little masks covering their faces, their weapons tucked in their belts, and their bodies all covered in mud and bits of foliage.

Anyone seeing these strange creatures would never have recognized them as Weasels.

Nobody needed to, for, in the next movement towards the Manor the leading Weasel touched a piece of wire across his path.

He froze to the spot, quite expecting alarm bells, flashing lights and whatever else a trip-wire would set off.

His little heart beat so quickly he could not feel his pulse.

No warning alarm rang and no lights came on.

He took a deep breath, composed himself and crawled carefully over the wire, taking care not to disturb it again.

Inside the Manor a piece of string, tied round Bastien's foot, gave one of his toes a tweak, waking him instantly.

The alarm had worked. The Weasels has arrived!

Bastien ran upstairs and pulled on another piece of string which ran from his bedroom to Bobby Bunny's house. A little bell tinkled by Bobby's bed.

He woke his sons. In a few seconds they were all dressed in strange hairy clothes.

Within a few minutes, four rather weird looking Rabbits left their warren, and headed towards Brock Manor, armed with dustbin lids and wooden sticks.

The Weasels had now entered the tunnel inside the Manor. It was covered in creepy, dusty cobwebs - homes for spiders!

They were beginning to get a little nervous.

They didn't like creepy-crawlies, and judging by the size of the cob-webs, these creepy-crawlies must be - well - enormous!

They managed to summon up enough courage to continue, and their shaking torches lit up the path ahead and revealed no creepy-crawlies in front of them.

It was now three o'clock and all the Weasels were inside the tunnel. The Bunny family arrived at the entrance of the tunnel a few minutes later, and Bastien was dressing in his study.

The leading Weasel arrived at a cross-roads in the tunnel and in his rush to enter the passage, had left the map with another Weasel. Now he wanted some directions.

He turned and asked the next Weasel behind him to pass a message down the line. "Pass the map up to me, please."

The next Weasel passed the message on. "Pass a mat up for his knees."

The next Weasel passed the message on. "Pass a hat before we freeze."

The next Weasel passed the message on. "Ask the chap what he needs."

The next Weasel passed the message on. "Let's go back for some cheese."

The next Weasel passed the message on. "Ahead is black, bit of a squeeze."

By the time the message had arrived at the Weasel who was carrying the map to the tunnels, the leading Weasel had explored one of the three directions which lay in front of him and it had been a dead end.

He was entering the second tunnel, when he heard a dull scuffling noise, coming from round the bend, just in front of him.

At that moment the scuffling noise materialized into - AN ENORMOUS LONG-LEGGED FURRY SPIDER which went "WO-OO-OO-OO".

The leading Weasel retreated back down the tunnel so quickly that he crashed into the next Weasel, who fell into the next one, and so on, and so on, until the whole line of Weasels had been knocked over.

The Weasels, already scared by the cobwebs and the dark, and frightened at just being bowled over, were terrified at the sound in front of them. They lost their nerves, got to their feet and turned as one, and bolted back down the tunnel.

They reached the entrance of the tunnel in a jabbering huddle, unsure quite what to do next, when four furry shapes appeared all around them, banging sticks on dustbin lids.

All records to reach the boundary wall of the manor must have been broken for, within five seconds flat, the Manor grounds were clear of Weasels.

The Bunnies were laughing and congratulating each other on the success of their efforts, when a huge eight-legged furry shape appeared at the entrance, making them turn suddenly quiet.

The furry shape put two of its furry legs to its head and started tugging at it. Off it came, revealing Bastien's beaming face.

"They won't be back in a hurry." he said, congratulating the Rabbits. Bobby Bunny agreed, shaking the Badger's outstretched hand.

"But then you can never be sure about those Weasels." he thought to himself.

The 'S' in Chester had been changed.

CHAPTER 5

THE NEWCOMERS

Bobby Bunny gazed at his pond. At last it was finished. Now he could start landscaping the rest of his garden.

He had received lots of information from mail-order companies on the subject, but he found that he could not buy the trees and shrubs locally, which he had seen in their glossy sales catalogues.

There were so many shrubs and trees, the names of which were quite unknown to Bobby, that he became completely confused with what to buy, so he asked a company for their suggestions and they had sent back a list of everything they thought he needed.

Bobby studied this list and was satisfied, because they were experts and their suggestions on garden layouts were far better than any ideas his efforts could hope to achieve. He decided to develop his garden in stages, to save spending too much money at any one time, otherwise he knew that Beattie would only tell him off, and so he decided to order a few plants and bushes at a time.

Soon word got round the villagers that Bobby Bunny was making a new garden and it wasn't long before many of them, keen to improve their own gardens, were seen peeping over his hedge, watching him while he worked. One such viewer was Bastien Badger from Brock Manor.

Bobby Bunny didn't mind anyone watching him for he was only too pleased to talk to them and answer their questions and give some advice when he could.

The company that Bobby ordered his plants from soon noticed the sudden demand for their goods, and decided to open a new branch in the town to attract more business. It so happened that Basil (Boots) Badger heard of this as, purely by chance, the company that Bobby had been ordering from, was partly owned by Basil's Aunt Blanche.

Soon a new Garden Centre opened near the Woodland Superstore, specialising in Plants, Trees, Gnomes, Pond Liners, Plastic Ponds, Water Pumps and equipment like forks, spades and rakes etc., for the 'you-too-can-do-it' gardener. A sparkling, newly painted sign was erected outside and it read: "WOODSIDE GARDEN CENTRE. Proprietors Ben and Ken Chester-Weasel."

Almost all the villagers went to this new Garden Centre to have a look around during the first week of its opening but, like all villagers, they were very wary of any newcomers to their village. The Chester-Weasels were smartly dressed Weasels with little moustaches. They were very slick in their manner and talk, and soon persuaded their customers to buy things they thought they wanted and many other things besides.

They gave talks at all the local meetings; the Gardening Club; Allotment Society and Women's Leisure Circle, and soon most of the listeners were convinced that they all needed a new garden.

They told their customers that everyone was buying trees and shrubs and the villagers, not wanting to feel left out, bought something, although not really sure what it was they had bought.

It wasn't long before the garden centre was doing a brisk business and the villagers soon noticed that the prices were beginning to rise.

Not everyone in the village could afford the higher prices and word was getting round the village that some of the items that the Chester-Weasels were selling, were not of a good quality.

Mitzi Mouse did not have much money to spend on her garden, and she was really proud of her roses, and felt that she had no real interest in any other types of plants.

The Chester-Weasels had heard of Mitzi's prize-winning roses, especially her blue ones, and offered to buy them all from her so that they could resell them in their Garden Centre.

Mitzi would not hear of such a thing. Sell her prize winning roses? Never! If her competitors bought them, she would, in effect, be competing with herself and she could not win the Buttercup that year. That would never do!

The Chester-Weasels were fascinated by the blue roses and were making plans to take some cuttings from Mitzi's garden, when a letter came from their head-office.

"Report on sales progress. Advise names and addresses of your customers," signed B. (B). B. (Nephew of a Shareholder)

Ken Chester-Weasel read the letter several times, frowned and handed it to his brother to read.

"What does he want to know the names and addresses of our customers for?" he asked his brother. "Who is he anyway?"

"Blessed if I know," said Ben, "we'd better give him what he wants, I suppose. After all, the shareholders do *own* the business, and we don't want any trouble from them, do we?"

The list of the names and addresses was sent off the next day and about a week later they received another letter which said, "Report immediately when you get a large order from Bastien Badger or someone living close to Brock Manor." B. (B). B.

A further two weeks passed and Bastien Badger asked to see Bobby Bunny's new garden. Bobby was so pleased that Bastien was interested in his garden, that he instructed Beattie to prepare afternoon tea on their new lawn as he was going to invite Bastien over, to show him his lovely new garden.

Bastien came two days later and spent the whole afternoon just walking round Bobby's garden, with a cup and saucer in his paws, from which he took the occasional sip, and asked all sorts of questions about Bobby's new garden and took particular interest in Bobby's pride and joy - his Garden Pond.

He asked countless questions on how he could build a Pond of his own, the best place to put it, what plants would be most suitable, and what sort of fish he should buy.

They were so busy, strolling about and talking, that they completely forgot about the food, and that quite upset Beattie.

Having spent all morning, cooking and preparing for Bastien's visit, how could they have ignored her efforts?

It was not many days later that Bastien sent Bobby Bunny to the Garden Centre to see the Chester-Weasels and Bobby bought a Pond Liner and ordered many plants on Bastien's behalf. A message was immediately sent to Head Office.

Aunt Blanche was delighted!

She wrote a letter and told Basil to make sure the letter was sent to the Chester-Weasels without delay.

The Chester-Weasels received the letter two days later and the envelope said: "CONFIDENTIAL - ONLY TO BE OPENED BY KEN CHESTER-WEASEL - URGENT"

Ken Chester-Weasel looked uneasily at the important looking letter and quickly put it down, on the table.

"Why don't you open it?" Ben asked, "It looks rather important to me. Hurry up, because we have a shop full of customers."

"Let's serve them first," Ken said, looking nervously at the letter, "then we'll open it. Customers are more important than letters."

Ben said, "It does say 'Urgent' so it must be important." But Ken would not open the letter and carried on serving his customers.

With the last customer gone, Ken had no choice but to open the letter.

"Dear Ken. Follow the instructions contained in this letter exactly and you will be well rewarded. Regards, Blanche Badger (Shareholder)"

He carefully read the instructions several times over.

Ken Chester-Weasel then visited Wilf Weasel who lived nearby, and read the contents of the letter from Blanche Badger to him.

"This could be our chance," muttered a thoughtful Wilf. "You make sure we get the job to plant all the shrubs and trees."

It was agreed.

The Garden Centre soon collected Bastien's order together, and when it was ready for delivery, Ken Chester-Weasel contacted Wilf Weasel and all the Weasel family arrived at the Garden Centre, with their equipment, in large sacks.

They met Bastien at the main gate of Brock Manor.

"Take it all into the garden," Bastien said, impatient to get his new pond and garden started, "You can make a start when Bobby Bunny comes back from his lunch in a few minutes."

The Weasels could not wait. They started unpacking their sacks, but it wasn't tools that they took out, but - weapons.

"Are we all ready?" asked Wilf. They were! "Right, let's get him!"

They rushed, as one, towards Bastien.

The Badger, taken completely by surprise, turned and ran to the Manor door, followed by the Weasels waving their weapons.

Bessie Beaver was just washing the Hall floor, as the first of the Weasels rushed into the Main Hall. They slipped over on the wet floor, then slid, crashing into the opposite wall.

Bessie was not pleased! She became very angry.

She grabbed the bucket containing the dirty water and emptied it all over the Weasels, then, grabbing her wet mop, she started lashing and splashing the mass of wriggling Weasels, and shouting. "You stupid Weasels, get you off my newly washed floor. I don't allow no-one on my floor until it's dry."

Some of the Weasels were dazed by hitting the wall, some shocked by being soaked and others bruised by Bessie's mop, but all were terrified, as they vividly recalled the other times they had tried to take the Manor by force.

They panicked and shrieked, as they wriggled about in a tangled heap on the wet floor, trying to get up, making Bessie even more angry.

"Get you off my nice clean floor!" she screamed at the top of her voice, and wielding her wet mop started attacking the Weasels again.

It was too much! The Weasels all dropped their weapons with a clatter and raised their arms in humiliated surrender.

"We give up, we give up," they wailed.

At that moment, Bobby Bunny returned from his lunch, just in time to see the surrender and help shepherd the Weasels into a large room and locked the door with a huge bolt.

When everything had quietened down and Bessie had rewashed the floor, Bastien called for Wilf Weasel and asked him for an explanation.

Wilf said that they needed land for new homes, and showed him the letters that he and the Chester-Weasels had received from Bastien's Aunt Blanche and his brother, Basil.

The letters told the Chester-Weasels to contact Wilf Weasel, and give him the gardening work at the Manor and capture Bastien. When this was achieved, they could have anything they wanted.

Bastien was horrified that his brother and Aunt would go to such despicable lengths to gain possession of the Manor.

He gave Bobby Bunny a note and said, "Tonight I want you to go to the Garden Centre."

In the morning the villagers that visited the garden Centre noticed that the sign had been changed.

The 'S' in Chester had been changed to an 'A'

It now said, 'WOODSIDE GARDEN CENTRE. Proprietors Ben and Ken CheAter-Weasels.'

The villagers soon heard about the attack on the Manor, saw the changed sign and remembered their own dealings with the Chester-Weasels and agreed that the name was really appropriate.

In the next few weeks, no-one visited the Garden Centre, and it had to close down due to lack of customers.

Bastien thanked the Weasels for their honesty and rewarded them with some of the land they needed, not all of it though, for they had been naughty Weasels and could not be entirely forgiven for doing other peoples' dirty work for them.

When Aunt Blanche discovered that the Weasels had failed yet again, and why the Garden Centre had been closed, she was so angry that her nephew, Basil, had to keep out of her way for several weeks.

She decided .... to write out her resignation.

CHAPTER 6

POOR BESSIE

A few months after the latest invasion by the Weasels, Bastien told Bobby Bunny that he was planning a huge party.

He wanted the garden to look lovely with all the plants and trees that he had bought from the Garden Centre some months before, and he wanted Beattie Bunny to organize an open day for all the villagers to visit the Manor for a special occasion.

What the special occasion was, he would not say. He would not even give a reason why Bessie Beaver, who usually organized everything, was not to be involved in it. The staff had their own thoughts on what the celebrations were for.

Was it for the victory over Basil and Aunt Blanche, the defeat of, and settlement with, the Weasels, or for Bastien inheriting the Manor? Could it be something to do with the CheAter-Weasels as they had become known?

Nobody dare ask Bessie's opinion, for she was becoming quite unreasonable and very moody. In fact, whenever she came near, conversations quickly changed to something quite different.

The party would be on Mid-summers day, a day guaranteed to be sunny and warm. and everyone was excitedly looking forward to it. Everyone that is, except Bessie Beaver.

She had overheard two servants talking about the party and was aware that any talk about it suddenly stopped whenever she appeared. When she asked Bastien why she had not been asked to organize it, he just told her that she had enough to do with running the household, and she was sent on meaningless errands, just to keep her out of the way.

Beattie Bunny dare not visit the manor to organize the party as she knew that Bessie would soon get the secret out of her, so she sent her orders on little secret notes to the staff. It was not easy keeping secrets from Bessie Beaver. She was continually peeping over shoulders at the notes and once or twice nearly read what was written on them.

This went on for several weeks and Bessie was becoming very upset. It was difficult for her to work properly, for she felt so sad at being left out.

She loved to organize summer parties. She had done them every year for Sir Regnault, but since Bastien had taken over the Manor - well - perhaps he wanted a younger person in her place.

The thought of that made her shudder. After being in service to the Badgers for thirty years, that was no way to be treated.

Perhaps she should offer her resignation and retire gracefully. Certainly not! She wasn't old enough to retire yet!

Perhaps she had done something wrong which Bastien had not mentioned. She couldn't recall anything.

What was wrong? The staff were so obviously avoiding her.

On the day before the party, Bessie thought she would have a last attempt at talking to Bastien to find out what the trouble was, but he would not spare her the time.

That evening, just after she had arrived home, she was so depressed, that she decided to put an end to the uncertainties and write out her resignation.

She sat down with pen and paper and tried to write the letter, but found it quite impossible to do, because of all the tears which welled in her eyes.

Some of them fell on the paper, smudging the wet ink, so that she had to start again.

On many occasions, her hand trembled, making her writing unreadable, so that she had to throw those letters away. She mis-spelt words, so had to rewrite *those* letters.

She looked around her home, through tearful eyes, and saw screwed-up pieces of paper everywhere.

She had not been able to complete one letter without a mistake.

So sad was she, that she went to bed without any tea, which made her feel worse, and she cried herself into a deep sleep.

The next day was a beautiful day. It was Mid-summer day and that was always a beautiful day. Perfect for any party.

The staff had the tables and chairs all set out on the lawn of the Manor early in the morning.

The tables had neat white tablecloths spread all over them, on which food and dishes, then more food and spoons and even more food and crackers, were laid, until it was nearly impossible to see the tablecloths.

Everyone was so busy that nobody noticed that Bessie had not come to work that morning.

She had been so sad the night before, that she had overslept from exhaustion, and by the time she had woken up, washed her tear-stained eyes, put on her make-up and had her breakfast, it was mid-morning and she still had a letter of resignation to write.

This time, as she wrote the letter out, she managed to hold back her few remaining tears, and completed it.

She would wait until lunch-time, then go to the Manor, hand the letter to Bastien and be home before the party started.

When she arrived at the Manor, there was nobody to be seen.

She searched everywhere. The doors were all locked. The windows were all closed tight, and she felt like putting her resignation letter through the letter box, but her pride insisted that she should hand it to Bastien himself.

This was the day of the party, somebody must be about as the tables were all laid out.

She walked all around the manor and finally went into the gardens where she could hear giggling coming from the lawn behind the large hedge.

As she looked round the corner of the hedge, Bastien suddenly jumped out in front of her, making Bessie jump back in fright.

"Come here," said Bastien quietly, "I'm sorry I frightened you, but we expected you earlier. We didn't think you would be late today, of all days."

Bessie felt terrible. She had never been this late for work before, and she began to feel a little guilty. Then she thought, 'but I am resigning today, so it really doesn't matter.'

To stop her running off, Bastien took her arm gently in his.

"Come with me." he said calmly, "I've got a surprise for you."

"I've got one for you too," snapped Bessie, instantly thrusting her letter of resignation into his free hand.

"What's this?" asked Bastien.

"It's my letter of resignation," said Bessie sadly, holding back the tears which were coming to her eyes.

"I'm sorry to do this on the day of the party," said Bessie, "but I've not been asked to organize it and everyone seems to have been avoiding me, so I thought it best not to ...."

"Would you mind if I didn't read it right this minute?" Bastien quickly butted in, "I don't think this is the appropriate time to be reading your letter at this moment."

"You please yourself," snapped Bessie, "but I'm going home now."

"Oh no you're not," commanded Bastien, still holding her arm, but a little more tightly now. You're coming with me."

Bessie resisted and tried to free her arm, but Bastien was much stronger than she was, and she could not break free from his grip.

He half-pulled, half-coaxed her to follow him onto the lawn.

A great cheer suddenly burst out all around them, and Bessie was immediately surrounded by all her staff and friends, all the villagers and all their children.

"You sit here," said Bastien, half afraid to let her go, in case she suddenly ran off.

Bessie had been gently led to the top table, to a seat right next to Bastien. She looked around her again. Everyone was cheering and clapping.

Bastien stood up and tried to quieten the cheering crowd by raising his arms.

It took several minutes to get the villagers quiet and then he started to speak.

"I would like to thank you all for coming to the party on this wonderful day. We could not have chosen a more beautiful day for this special occasion."

"It is not often that we have the opportunity to hold a celebration like this and it is a great shame that my father is no longer here with us, to share it."

"As you all know, this special day celebrates thirty years of dedicated service to Brock Manor and the Badger family, by a someone who is well know and well respected by us all."

Bessie pricked-up her ears. *She* had worked at the Manor for thirty years. What's all this about? What was going on?

"It is very difficult, at the best of times, to keep a secret from Bessie Beaver, and it has been almost impossible to keep the reason for this special party secret, but I must congratulate you all for the wonderful way you have achieved it."

"Being the person she is, she would not have allowed us to honor her in this way, so Bessie - he turned towards her, - I should like to present you with this special medal, the S.E.M., in appreciation of your loyalty and dedication to the Manor."

Bastien produced a beautiful claret coloured box from one of his pockets, and opened it up to reveal a sparkling round silver medal with a shiny blue ribbon, nestling in the lovely silk lining of the case. It shone in the sun, almost matching the beaming smile that had slowly appeared on Bessie's face.

Bastien removed the 'Service of Excellence Medal' from its protective case and pinned it to Bessie's pinafore, amid a deluge of cheering, clapping and shouting.

Bessie pinched herself. She must be dreaming!

No she wasn't, because she had felt the pinch. *That* was real enough.

She winced at the sharp pain, shook her head and stood up.

The noise of the cheering, clapping and shouting did not stop, so she had to sit down again, because she almost fell over with emotion.

Eventually Bastien calmed the guests, sufficiently for Bessie to say a few works.

"I-I-I really don't know what to say," she said shyly. "It is such a surprise. I thought I was not wanted at the Manor any more, because everyone has gone out of their way to avoid me, and it made me feel quite unwelcomed."

A wave of embarrassed giggling and concealed chuckling broke out amongst the guests, which quickly stopped when they realized they were being rude.

She continued. I spent the whole of last night trying to write out my resignation as I was so sad. Now I feel *so* important, like a queen for the day, with this wonderful medal which I really don't deserve as I was only doing my job."

"I hope you", - she turned to Bastien, - "will allow me to stay at the Manor and will give me back my letter of resignation."

Bastien nodded in an 'of course I will' manner.

"I think that I had better sit down," said Bessie, "so that the party can proceed, but, once again, thank you all so much for this wonderful day. It really is one I shall never forget, and I will treasure it for the rest of my life.

She sat down amid a thunderous roar of clapping and cheering, and the noise of a window breaking, which only a few heard. Those that did hear it were too involved in the celebrations to take any notice.

Beattie Bunny had organised the meal well, with lots of crackers with little riddles in them, which everyone pulled, then put on the paper hats and giggled at the ridiculous riddles which fell out the crackers.

One read out: "When is a door not a door? - When its ajar!"

Another read: "What can go up a chimney down, but cannot come down a chimney up? - an umbrella!"

Another read: "What time is it when a clock strikes thirteen? - Time it was mended!"

Another read: "Why didn't the cat open the door when it was told to? - Because the cat said 'Me-how'?

Another read: "What does a Piggy put on grazes and scratches? - 'OINK'-MENT.

There were so many things to do, and when all the food had been eaten, and all the drink had been drunk, all the guests tried their luck at the tombolas and other side events.

One was a rusty old chain dangling in some dirty water. There was a notice which said. 'See the Water 'Otter. Place a penny in the slot and pull the chain'.

Some of the younger children could not see the funny side of the joke when they placed their penny in the slot, pulled the chain and a *rusty old kettle* emerged from the water, and there were a few tears as the children had expected to see a rare animal.

"Well it *is* a water hotter. You *do* heat water in it don't you"? said their parents, but the children did not see the joke.

Another event was guessing the number of beans in a bottle.

Then you could throw darts at playing cards. If you hit the coloured shapes two times out of three, then you would win a prize.

There was a raffle for some of Beattie Bunny's cakes.

There was a prize for blowing up the biggest balloon, but this contest had to be stopped, as some of the smaller children were being lifted off the ground by the balloon they were blowing up, and were floating away.

It was the most wonderful party ever, and it went on until quite late in the evening.

With the children all getting tired and sleepy, their parents knew it was time to take them home for their beds, so the party gradually came to an end.

Bessie insisted on helping clear away the dishes, tables and chairs after the party, but she was ordered off home. After all, it was *her* special day.

By the time everything was cleared away, it was getting quite dark and everybody had been too busy washing and drying up the dishes to notice the broken window near the back door of the Manor and the strong smell of an unusual perfume .....

...to be continued in Book 2 "PROBLEMS AT BROCK MANOR"

Printed in the United States
by Baker & Taylor Publisher Services